Gilbert in the Snow

Written by Michèle Dufresne

Contents

PIONEER VALLEY EDUCATIONAL PRESS, INC.

CHAPTER 1
Come and Play

It was winter. Gilbert was bored.
There was nothing to do
during the winter.
The kids in the neighborhood
didn't come over to the farm
to play during the winter.
Gilbert was tired of being
in the barn.

Just then, Gilbert heard something
outside the barn.
Some of the kids were here!
"Can Gilbert come out and play?"
he heard a girl say.

It was Amber! She was talking to the farmer. She wanted him to come out and play!

"Gilbert doesn't like the cold very much," the farmer told the kids. "I don't think he'll come out."

"I can put my scarf on him," said Amber.
"That will help him stay warm!"

Gilbert got up
and walked outside.
"Gilbert!" said the kids.
"Come and play with us.
It will be fun. We haven't
seen you in a long time!"

The farmer patted Gilbert.
"Look, Gilbert!" she said.
"Here is Amber, Ashley,
and John to play with you!"

"Oink, oink," said Gilbert.

"Come on," said the kids.
"Come and play!"

Yuck! The snow was wet
and cold! But Gilbert was bored.
He wanted to play. He could do it.
Gilbert walked around a little.
It wasn't so bad.
It wasn't too cold. Yes, he would
play with the kids in the snow.

CHAPTER 2
Snow Fun

Amber put her scarf on Gilbert. "That will keep you warm," she told him.

"Come on, let's play," said John.

"What should we do?" asked Amber.

"Let's make snow angels," suggested John.

The kids lay down and began making angels in the snow.

"Come on, Gilbert,
make a snow pig," laughed Amber.
But Gilbert was not going to
lie down in the snow. It was wet!
It was cold!

"Now what?" asked John.
"Gilbert doesn't want
to make snow angels."

Ashley looked around.
"We could make a snow fort,"
she said. "That would be fun."

The kids pushed the snow into
piles to make a wall for the fort.
"This is awesome!" said Ashley.

"Do you like our fort, Gilbert?"
asked John.

Gilbert didn't like the fort.
It was cold in the fort.
It was wet in the fort.
"Oink, oink," said Gilbert.

CHAPTER 3
Warm Mush

"What else can we do?" asked John.

"We could go sledding," suggested Amber. "Maybe Gilbert likes to go sledding."

The kids got a sled. "Look, Gilbert," said Amber. "We can go down the hill on the sled."

Gilbert looked at the sled.
He was **not** getting on
that sled. He turned to go back
to his warm, dry barn.

"Come back!" said Ashley.
"It will be awesome!"

"We need to get him up the hill," said John.

"Come on, Gilbert," urged the kids.

They tried to push Gilbert
up the hill.
"Push harder!" said John.
The kids pushed and pushed.
Gilbert would not budge.
He was not going up the hill.

"Let's get him on the sled.
We can pull him up the hill,"
said John.
The kids tried to push Gilbert
onto the sled.
"Push harder!" said John.
The three kids pushed and pushed.
Gilbert would not budge.

Gilbert was not going up the hill.

"Let's show him how much fun
it is," said Amber.

The kids went up the hill
and came sliding down.
"Look!" they yelled to Gilbert.
"Gilbert, this is so much fun.
Now it's your turn!
You will like this, Gilbert.
It is fun sledding down the hill!"

Gilbert didn't like the sled.
He didn't like the snow.
He just didn't like winter.
He wanted to go back to his
warm, dry barn.

"Who wants hot chocolate?"
called the farmer.
The children came running,
and Gilbert followed.
"Here's the hot chocolate,"
said the farmer.
"And some warm mush
for you, Gilbert."

"Warm mush! Now this is more
like it," thought Gilbert.

"Yum," said the kids.
"Thanks! We love hot chocolate!"

"Oink, oink!" said Gilbert.

Gilbert ate his mush and then
walked into the barn and lay down
in the hay with his soft blankets.
It was warm and dry in the barn.
He didn't like making snow angels
or snow forts.
He didn't like sledding.
But he did like the warm mush.
In the spring, he would go
back out and play with the kids.
The barn was the best place
to be in the winter.